Tyrell's Big Move

ILLUSTRATED BY
JIAQI ZHOU

TALIK BARBER, SYNIA ROBINSON,
JADA BROWN, AND TEMIL WHIPPLE

Reach Incorporated | Washington, DC

Shout Mouse Press

Reach Education, Inc. / Shout Mouse Press
Published by
Shout Mouse Press, Inc.

Shout Mouse Press is a nonprofit writing and publishing program dedicated to amplifying unheard voices. This book was produced through Shout Mouse writing workshops and in collaboration with Shout Mouse artists and editors..

Shout Mouse Press empowers writers from marginalized communities to tell their own stories in their own voices and, as published authors, to act as agents of change. In partnership with other nonprofit organizations serving communities in need, we are building a catalog of inclusive, mission-driven books that engage reluctant readers as well as open hearts and minds.

Learn more and see our full catalog at www.shoutmousepress.org.

Copyright © 2018 Reach Education, Inc.
ISBN-13: 978-1945434952 (Shout Mouse Press, Inc.)
ISBN-10: 1945434953

For anyone who has had to let go.

On a sunny Friday afternoon, Tyrell came home from school. He was excited to tell his mom about show-and-tell. That day he had showed off his favorite toy. Everybody loved his robot that transformed into a car.

"Wow, I want one," said Donny, who usually had all the coolest toys.

Tyrell felt like the man.

When he walked in the door, his mom was waiting with his all-time favorite snack... a glass of milk and that special chocolate with caramel in the middle!

He was so excited he forgot to take off his shoes and backpack.

He took his first bite. Then he remembered that the last time he got his special snack, there was bad news.

"Mom," Tyrell said, "What's going on?"

"Well...I have something to tell you."

Tyrell felt like there were a billion butterflies in his stomach.

"Listen, peanut. I have bad news. We have to move out by the end of the week."

"The end of the week!?"

"I'm so sorry. Everybody has to move. Our building was sold. They're going to tear it down and build something new."

Tyrell stormed to his room and slammed the door, something he never did.

He had lived in this apartment his whole life.

He could not imagine living anywhere else.

"This is my home," he said.

Tyrell did not know whether to be sad or mad about the news. He was going to miss the neighborhood.

What about Mrs. Windell and her yappy dog Tuff?

He sure would miss Mr. Graham. Every Friday he brought Tyrell his favorite popsicles.

Tyrell fell asleep feeling like he might never be happy again.

That night he dreamed that everything and everyone he ever loved floated away.

In the morning, Tyrell woke up feeling down.

His mom came in with a big breakfast and a smile.

"I have a surprise for you, Peanut! Breonna's coming for the weekend!"

Tyrell perked up. Breonna was his favorite cousin!

They ate their yummy breakfast and Tyrell waited and waited for the doorbell to ring.

Once his cousin arrived, Tyrell forgot about the bad
news. He and Breonna had a great time.
They had a pillow fight...

They ate dinosaur-shaped chicken nuggets...

They drank fruit punch!

But when it was time to go to sleep, Tyrell remembered last night's sadness. He had so many questions.

Why did those people want to tear down this building?

Wasn't it great the way it was?

Was he going to have to go to a new school?

Was he going to make new friends?

Were he and Breonna ever going to see each other again?

Tyrell started to cry.

"What's the matter?" asked Breonna.

"It's not fair," sobbed Tyrell. "My mom says we have to move."

"Oh yeah, I heard Mommy and Auntie talking about it. But you're going just across town, right?" said Breonna.

Tyrell kept crying.

"It's OK," she said. "You will make lots of friends wherever you go. And I will always come visit you."

Breonna gave him a big hug.

"Hey!" she said. "I have an idea. Let's go visit all your favorite places this week!"

This made Tyrell feel better.

He did want to see his favorite places one more time...

When they woke up the next morning, Breonna suggested they go to the park. Tyrell loooooved those swings. The swings at his park went very, very high.

Tyrell swung his legs as hard as he could.

He soared above the swingset, over the trees, and into the sky.

That evening they went to his favorite restaurant, Noodle Ole. He ordered his favorite meal, spaghetti with meatballs shaped like stars.

"I sure will miss these meatballs," Tyrell said to Breonna.

"Hey, Ty," said C.J., his favorite waitress.

They did their secret handshake.

On Monday, he walked to school with Breonna.

He knew that day he was going to learn about fractions.

"Breonna, do you think I'll ever see Mr. P again?" he asked.
"He's my favorite teacher."

"Ty, you'll have plenty of great teachers along the way!"

On Tuesday after school he went with Breonna to the library. They had puppet shows there every week. He loved when the puppet masters did Little Red Riding Hood. When the Big Bad Wolf came out dressed as Grandma, Tyrell laughed and laughed.

On Wednesday, Tyrell's father picked him up from school. Tyrell only saw his father once a week.

"What's the matter, Peanut? You don't seem like yourself," said Dad.

"You know that we're moving?"

"Yeah, I know. Don't worry. No matter where you go, I will find a way to see you."

At least I don't need to worry about that, Tyrell thought.

Thursday

On Thursday, it was time to pack up.
Tyrell's mom said he couldn't take all of his toys.
He had to choose the top three.

Tyrell's

First, he chose his favorite, the
robot that turns into a car.

Then, he chose his race car night light. His dad gave it to him when he was younger. He's used it ever since.

Finally, he packed up his favorite stuffed animal. It was a bear that he had all his life. Tyrell needed the bear to go to sleep. He hoped it would remind him of home.

After he was done packing, Tyrell said out loud, "I'm going to miss this room."

His mom was standing in the doorway.

"I know you're still feeling down, Peanut. But trust me, everything is going to be okay."

She sat down on his bed and he sat beside her.

"You know," she said, "I moved around a lot when I was younger. I had to make new friends. But I kept the old ones, too. It might be hard at first but you'll get the hang of it. You're great at making friends."

Friday

Friday was moving day.

Tyrell knew it was his last day living in the neighborhood. But he was not as scared as he used to be. He felt a little more confident after talking to his mom, his dad, and his cousin.

Maybe it won't be so bad, he thought.

He climbed into the moving truck with his mom.

Just then, someone shouted his name.

It was Breonna! And she had something in her hand.

It was a photo collage.

It had pictures of Tyrell in all of his favorite places.

"I made this so you never forget where you came from," Breonna said.

Tyrell hugged Breonna really tightly.

Then it was time to go.

NOODLE OLE!

Mr. Graham's popsicles

↗ yappy Tuff ☺

Your
FAVORITE
Swing
↙

Tyrell and his mom climbed into the truck. Breonna waved as they drove away. Even after Breonna was out of sight, Tyrell kept looking out the window.

"Peanut," said his mom. "The important thing to remember is that home is just a place where you feel loved. You can take that with you."

Tyrell thought about it. His mom was right.

He leaned against her and took a deep breath.

He was ready for all the new things coming his way.

A few months later...

↗ Tyrell
the painter

↖ Breonna's
Visit

@ the new ↗
swimming pool !
☺

My <u>favorite</u> Slide !!!

New friends at school!

About the Authors

Talik Barber

is a junior at Dunbar Senior High School. He loves to play sports like football and basketball. His dream is to become a licensed barber or an NFL football player. In his free time, he likes spending time with his family and friends. Writing his first children's book with Reach and Shout Mouse was a fantastic experience because he's never done it before and he believes it's important to explore new things.

Jada Brown

is a senior at Thurgood Marshall Academy. She works at Six Flags America. In her spare time she likes to eat and skateboard. This is her first children's book. The experience was fun and challenging. Writing this book showed her that she can work with other people to put something good together, which she thought she couldn't do. She hopes readers will relate to the story and that this book helps kids learn how to read.

Synia Robinson

is a sophomore at Ballou Senior High School. She loves to eat and read. She like mystery books. This is her first children's book with Reach and Shout Mouse Press. Her dream is to become a lawyer.

Temil Whipple

is a senior at Dunbar Senior High School. She is an outgoing young lady who loves to write. Temil plans on going to college and pursuing her goals. This is her second children's book. Her first was *Spanky The Pup: All Dogs Must Go* (2016). She has also written two other Shout Mouse books, the young adult novels *Trinitoga* (2014) and *The Day Tajon Got Shot* (2017).

Sarai Johnson served as Story Coach for this book.

Hayes Davis served as Head Story Coach for this year's series.

About the Illustrator

Jiaqi Zhou

Originally from Shanghai, China, Jiaqi came to United States by herself when she was 18 to pursue her dreams. She graduated from Virginia Commonwealth University with a BFA in Communication Arts in 2017. Currently, she is continuing her art adventure in New Jersey as a freelance illustrator and designer. She loves to read, write, and illustrate stories, and she is passionate about delivering feeling and emotions in her work. You can see more of her work at jiaqizhou.com

Writers and artists at work

Acknowledgments

For the sixth summer in a row, teens from Reach Incorporated were issued a challenge: compose original children's books that will both educate and entertain young readers. Specifically, these teens were asked to create inclusive stories that reflect the realities of their communities, so that every child has the opportunity to relate to characters on the page. And for the sixth summer in a row, these teens have demonstrated that they know their audience, they believe in their mission, and they take pride in the impact they can make on young lives.

Thirteen writers spent the month of July brainstorming ideas, generating potential plots, writing, revising, and providing critiques. Authoring quality books is challenging work, and these authors have our immense gratitude and respect: Talik, Synia, Jada, Temil, Trevon, Kahliya, De'Asia, India, Essence, Malik, Brittany, Dartavius, and Don'nayah.

These books represent a collaboration between Reach Incorporated and Shout Mouse Press, and we are grateful for the leadership provided by members of both teams. From Reach, John Gass contributed meaningfully to discussions and morale, and the Reach summer program leadership of Luisa Furstenberg-Beckman kept us organized and well-equipped. From the Shout Mouse Press team, we thank Head Story Coach Hayes Davis, who oversaw this year's workshops, and Story Coaches Holly Bass, Sarai Johnson, Barrett Smith, and Eva Shapiro for bringing both fun and insight to the project. We can't thank enough illustrators Jiaqi Zhou, Liu Light, West Cahall, and India Valle for bringing these stories to life with their beautiful artwork. Finally, Amber Colleran brought a keen eye and important mentorship to the project as the series Art Director and book designer. We are grateful for the time and talents of these writers and artists!

Finally, we thank those of you who have purchased books and cheered on our authors. It is your support that makes it possible for these teen authors to engage and inspire young readers. We hope you smile as much while you read as these teens did while they wrote.

Mark Hecker,
Reach Incorporated

Kathy Crutcher,
Shout Mouse Press

About Reach Incorporated

Reach Incorporated develops grade-level readers and capable leaders by preparing teens to serve as tutors and role models for younger students, resulting in improved literacy outcomes for both.

Founded in 2009, Reach recruits high school students to be elementary school reading tutors. Elementary school students average 1.5 grade levels of reading growth per year of participation. This growth – equal to that created by highly effective teachers – is created by high school students who average more than two grade levels of growth per year of program participation.

As skilled reading tutors, our teens noticed that the books they read with their students did not reflect their reality. As always, we felt the best way we could address this issue was to let our teen tutors author new books themselves. Through our collaboration with Shout Mouse Press, these teens create engaging stories with diverse characters that invite young readers to explore the world through words. By purchasing our books, you support student-led, community-driven efforts to improve educational outcomes in the District of Columbia.

Learn more at reachincorporated.org.

CPSIA information can be obtained
at www.ICGtesting.com
Printed in the USA
LVHW071704100320
649608LV00019B/586

9 781945 434952